W9-BCD-670

The Boxcar Children Mysteries

The Movie Star Mystery
The Mystery of the Pirate's Map
The Ghost Town Mystery
The Mystery of the Black Raven
The Mystery in the Mall
The Mystery in New York
The Gymnastics Mystery
The Poison Frog Mystery
The Mystery of the Empty Safe
The Home Run Mystery
The Great Bicycle Race Mystery
The Mystery of the Wild Ponies
The Mystery in the Computer Game
The Mystery at the Crooked House
The Hockey Mystery
The Mystery of the Midnight Dog
The Mystery of the Screech Owl
The Summer Camp Mystery
The Copycat Mystery
The Haunted Clock Tower Mystery
The Mystery of the Tiger's Eye
The Disappearing Staircase Mystery
The Mystery on Blizzard Mountain
The Mystery of the Spider's Clue
The Candy Factory Mystery
The Mystery of the Mummy's Curse
The Mystery of the Star Ruby
The Stuffed Bear Mystery
The Mystery of Alligator Swamp
The Mystery at Skeleton Point
The Tattletale Mystery
The Comic Book Mystery
The Great Shark Mystery
The Ice Cream Mystery
The Midnight Mystery

The Mystery in the Fortune Cookie
The Black Widow Spider Mystery
The Radio Mystery
The Mystery of the Runaway Ghost
The Finders Keepers Mystery
The Mystery of the Haunted Boxcar
The Clue in the Corn Maze
The Ghost of the Chattering Bones
The Sword of the Silver Knight
The Game Store Mystery
The Mystery of the Orphan Train
The Vanishing Passenger
The Giant Yo-Yo Mystery
The Creature in Ogopogo Lake
The Rock 'n' Roll Mystery
The Secret of the Mask
The Seattle Puzzle
The Ghost in the First Row
The Box That Watch Found
A Horse Named Dragon
The Great Detective Race
The Ghost at the Drive-In Movie
The Mystery of the Traveling Tomatoes
The Spy Game
The Dog-Gone Mystery
The Vampire Mystery
Superstar Watch
The Spy in the Bleachers
The Amazing Mystery Show
The Clue in the Recycling Bin
Monkey Trouble

MONKEY TROUBLE

created by
GERTRUDE CHANDLER WARNER

Illustrated by Robert Papp

ALBERT WHITMAN & Company
Chicago, Illinois

Library of Congress Cataloging-in-Publication Data is available.

Monkey Trouble
Created by Gertrude Chandler Warner;
Illustrated by Robert Papp.

ISBN: 978-0-8075-5239-1 (hardcover)
ISBN: 978-0-8075-5240-7 (paperback)

10 9 8 7 6 5 4 3 2 1 LB 16 15 14 13 12 11

Cover art by Robert Papp.

For information about Albert Whitman & Company,
visit our web site at www.albertwhitman.com.

Contents

MONKEY TROUBLE

CHAPTER 1

At the Zoo

"Henry, I will be back to pick you all up at exactly three o'clock," Grandfather Alden told his fourteen-year-old grandson as he dropped his four grandchildren off at the zoo. Henry was the oldest of the Alden children, and he always looked out for his younger siblings.

Henry checked his watch. "Perfect," he said. "We'll meet you here, right after the tour is over."

"I'm so glad we signed up for the spring

break two-day zoo tour. It's going to take both days to see all the new animals," said twelve-year-old Jessie. As Jessie spoke, she pulled her straight brown hair into a ponytail. "The article I read online said there were twenty different kinds of babies born at the zoo this spring. Giraffes, zebras, penguins, monkeys—"

"Ohhh!" interrupted Jessie's sister, Violet. "Baby monkeys are so cute! I can't wait to see them." The ten-year-old rushed forward and gave Grandfather a big, tight hug. "Thank you so very much for bringing us today."

Jessie, Violet, Henry, and Benny Alden lived with their grandfather. After their parents died, they ran away and hid in a railroad boxcar. They'd heard that James Alden was mean, and even though they'd never met him, they were afraid to live with him. But when Grandfather finally found them, it turned out that he wasn't mean at all. As a matter of fact, he was a kind and generous man.

When the Aldens moved in with Grandfather, he let them bring along the dog they found on their adventures—a wire-haired terrier named Watch. Now the boxcar was a clubhouse in their backyard.

Grandfather handed Violet her lunch bag. Violet put the sack into a colorful patchwork tote bag that she'd decorated with puff paints.

Jessie took her own lunch and went to the car's trunk to put on her backpack. She liked to write about things she saw, so she had tucked a new notebook into the side pocket. "I can't wait to get started," she said.

"Me neither," said Benny. At six years old, Benny was the youngest of the Alden children.

Henry took his own lunch sack from Grandfather, then pulled Benny's pack out of the trunk with a grunt. "Wow, Benny," he said. "This is very heavy for a six-year-old! What do you have in here? Rocks?"

Benny smiled and licked his lips hungrily. "Better than rocks." He put out his arms so Henry could heave the pack onto his small shoulders. "I have snacks! Lots and lots of snacks."

Violet, Jessie, and Henry all laughed. They knew that Benny's stomach was a bottomless pit.

Grandfather held up Benny's brown lunch sack. "I guess you don't need this, then."

"Oh, but I do!" Benny said, taking the bag. "Lunch is the most delicious meal of the day." Benny paused. "I mean, besides breakfast and dinner."

Everyone laughed again.

Benny asked Henry to put the lunch bag in the outside pocket of his backpack.

"I'm ready!" he declared. Then he pointed at the entrance to the zoo. "Let's go!"

Grandfather waved goodbye as the children went on their way. With Benny in the lead, Jessie, Violet, and Henry followed him to the ticket line. After Jessie paid, they went straight to a small red barn. There was a sign hanging in front: Greenfield Zoo Education Center, it read. Benny opened the door to the barn, and they all went inside.

There were no animals in this barn. Instead, there were twenty metal folding chairs set up in a circle, a chalkboard, and lots of posters of animals on the walls.

"I'm so excited," Benny gushed. "Kids from all over Greenfield will be at this zoo tour. I can't wait to make new friends."

"I hope there will be some kids we already know from school," Violet added. "That would be nice, too."

After putting their lunches in a cooler and their bags and backpacks in cubbies, the Alden children hurried to sit down. The tour was about to begin.

Jessie waved across the circle to a few kids she knew from school.

"Hi Sophie!" Benny said as a tall blond girl walked in.

"Hi Benny." Sophie Webb was fourteen—Henry's age. She was a very fast swimmer. In elementary school, she had won so many races on the Greenfield Swim Team that now she was training with a professional coach. That meant Sophie didn't go to school with Henry anymore. Tutors taught her school subjects at home every morning. In the afternoons, Sophie trained in the pool.

Benny leaned over to Violet. "Sophie is amazing," he whispered.

"I know," Violet whispered back. "Someday she'll probably be swimming in the Olympics. Wouldn't it be incredible if she won a gold medal?"

A pair of twin boys sat next to Henry. Benny didn't know them, but they said that their names were Matthew and Griffin Cho. They told Benny that they were six years old.

"Just like me!" Benny said happily.

"Here comes the tour guide," Jessie said. She ruffled Benny's hair and reminded him to pay attention.

"Hello," greeted a young man with dark hair and glasses. He was carrying a bag that had the zoo's name printed on it. "My name is Rob Newton." He set the bag on the ground near his feet. "I'll be showing you many amazing baby animals over the next two days. I'm studying to be a zoologist, so I can tell you all about them."

Benny's hand shot up. "What's a zoologist?" he asked.

"That's a good question," Mr. Newton told Benny. "I learn all about animals. I study the differences between those that live in the wild and the ones that are in cages at the zoo."

Benny's eyes lit up. "Can I be a zoologist someday, too?"

Mr. Newton grinned. "Sure. You can study zoology in college."

"Oh," Benny said with a big sigh. "I don't think I can wait that long."

Mr. Newton saw the disappointment on Benny's face. "Well, I need a helper during the tour," he said. "Would you like to be my assistant zoologist today?"

"I'd love it! Thanks!" Benny jumped out of his seat, excited to help.

"This spring break tour group is very lucky! Because of all the new animal babies, the zoo has decided to have a photo contest—just for you!" Mr. Newton pulled a small cardboard camera out of his bag. It was the disposable kind. They had a digital camera at home, but the Aldens had seen this kind of camera at a wedding last summer. These cameras were made so that a person could use up the film quickly, develop the pictures, and then recycle the cardboard camera.

"Cameras cost five dollars," Mr. Newton explained. "At the end of our tour tomorrow, I will collect them and get the pictures developed. The photos will be judged by the Greenfield Zoo's zoologists. Then, tomorrow night we will have a pizza party to announce the winner. The first-prize winner will get their picture in the zoo newsletter. That person will also get a year-long free pass to the zoo!"

Everyone cheered.

"A pizza party!" Benny said. He rushed over to Henry. "I don't think my tummy can wait until tomorrow evening."

Henry laughed. "It definitely makes sense to have the party at the end of the tour, Benny. Your tummy will just have to wait."

"Hang in there," Benny said to his belly with a sigh. be

"It would fun to take pictures for the photo contest," Violet said.

"I wonder . . ." Henry looked at Jessie. She was carrying the change from the zoo tickets. "Do we have enough money to buy a camera?" he asked her.

Jessie pulled out the cash and counted what was left. "We have five dollars and thirty-seven cents," she reported.

"Terrific!" Violet said, taking the money. "We can get one camera and share it."

"But what about the prize?" Jessie asked. "The winner gets just one zoo pass."

"We can take turns with that, too," Henry said.

"Can I take the first picture?" Benny asked. "Please?"

"Of course," said Jessie.

"And after that, whoever sees something interesting can have a turn," Henry said.

Violet went to buy the camera, and Benny, proud to be Mr. Newton's assistant, went to help him sell them.

"Here," Benny said, giving Violet the camera. "Don't forget, I get to take the first photo!"

"I won't forget," Violet said, handing Mr. Newton the money.

Violet recognized Blake Morrison, the photographer for the school newspaper, by his bright red hair. He was standing in line behind her. "I'll need two cameras," Blake told Benny. He held out a crisp ten-dollar bill.

"Two?" Annika Gentry, a girl in the grade below Violet and Blake, spun around. She was petite with short, brown hair. She held up the camera she just bought. "Everyone should only get one."

Annika's tone was curiously angry. Violet and Benny both stopped to listen.

"I'm a professional photographer," Blake told her. "I need two cameras."

"You aren't a professional," Annika replied.

"Am too." Blake took a step toward her. "I take pictures for the school paper. You don't."

"I want to! But you won't let me," Annika said.

"Yes. I'm the only photographer and the editor, too. I get to decide what jobs everyone has for the newspaper," Blake said. "You can write the horoscopes if you want."

Annika gave Blake an angry look. "If I'm on the paper, I want to be a photographer!" She stomped her foot. Then she turned to Mr. Newton. "Please don't sell Blake two cameras. It won't be fair to the rest of us. He'll have twice as many chances to win the contest."

Mr. Newton considered what Annika was saying. He pushed up his glasses and then looked over a sheet of paper that had the contest rules on it. "Sorry, Annika," he told her at last. "The rules don't say anything about a camera limit."

Blake snorted at Annika while Benny handed him two cameras.

"Listen," Blake said to Annika. "If you win this photo contest, I'll let you be a photographer on the newspaper staff. But if you lose, you have to promise to stop bugging me about it. Deal?"

Annika thought about it for a second, staring at her one and only camera. Then she looked over at the two cameras that Blake held.

"You can buy a second one tomorrow if you want," Mr. Newton told Annika.

"That's okay," Annika said to Mr. Newton. "I'm such a good photographer that I don't need two cameras."

Annika turned to Benny, who was still standing nearby listening. "You're our witness, okay?" Annika said to Benny. "You heard what Blake said. If I win, I get to take pictures for the school newspaper."

"Okay," Benny said. "I'm a good witness. I witness stuff all the time." Then he asked, "Umm. What's a witness?"

"It's someone who makes sure everyone keeps a deal," Blake said.

"Got it!" Benny said smiling.

Annika and Blake shook hands to seal the agreement.

"Excuse me," Matthew and Griffin Cho said to Benny. "We want to buy a camera too, please."

"Sure!" Benny handed a camera to the Cho twins. "Good luck to you both!"

Mr. Newton finished selling cameras.

"I want everyone to put on sunscreen," he said. "We are leaving the Education Center in two minutes."

Jessie and Violet were putting lotion on their faces when they saw Sophie come up to Blake at the sunscreen table. "Can I borrow one of your cameras?" she asked.

"Huh?" Blake looked at Sophie with a confused expression. "Why don't you buy one of your own?"

"Preparing for the Olympics is really expensive," Sophie explained. "My parents don't have any leftover money. They got me the ticket to come on the tour, but I can't buy anything." She pointed at Blake's hand. "So can I use your extra camera?"

"No," Blake said, putting both his cameras into his over-the-shoulder bag. "I am doubling my chances to win first place in the contest. I can't share." And with that, he turned and walked off. Sophie stared at the back of Blake's head as he went.

"You can share with us if you want," Henry offered.

"No, thanks," Sophie said. "I really wanted a camera that I could use by myself all day."

Mr. Newton walked over to the small red barn's exit. He told everyone to gather by the sign that read, "Greenfield Zoo Education Center." "Come on, everyone," he said. "The baby animals are waiting."

Mr. Newton handed Benny a long pole with a red flag that said tour on top.

"If you get lost, look for the flag," Mr. Newton said to all the students. He told Benny to walk next to him at the front of the group.

"Off we go," Mr. Newton said. He pointed the way out of the barn and toward the baby penguins.

Violet hung back with Henry and Jessie as the group headed out. "Annika and Blake really weren't getting along," she said. "I hope they don't argue with each other all day. That would upset everyone on the zoo tour."

"They won't," Jessie said to her sister. "All the cute zoo babies will put everybody in a good mood."

Henry laughed. "It's going to be a perfect day," he said.

Violet hoped her brother and sister were right.

CHAPTER 2

Beautiful Babies

"Did I miss anything?" Nico Guerraro, a boy from Jessie's class, came rushing up to the group. He was panting hard.

"We're just starting," Jessie told Nico. She explained about the cameras and the contest. "You should get a camera now if you want to enter."

Nico patted his pants pockets. "Can't," he said. "No money. I was running so late, I even forgot my lunch." He rubbed his belly. "I know I'm going to be hungry later."

"Don't worry," Benny said. He pointed at his full backpack. "I have loads of snacks with me. You can have some."

At that, Nico smiled. "Great. I'll help carry it if it gets too heavy." Then Nico frowned. "Now if only I had a camera," he said. He pushed his shaggy black hair off his face.

"Don't ask Blake for one," Sophie said. "He's got two, but he won't share."

"And it's not fair," Annika added, stepping up next to Sophie. She was much shorter than Sophie, so Annika looked up and said firmly, "He's a contest-cheating camera hog."

"Am not!" Blake's face was as red as his hair when he turned toward Annika. "Mr. Newton told me that I could have two. You heard him. I'm not breaking any rules."

It looked like a fight was about to begin. But at that moment, Mr. Newton made an announcement. "The baby penguins are right over here. Everyone follow me and Benny, please."

With a toss of her short brown hair, Annika hurried ahead to walk with Benny.

Sophie moved to the back of the group. Nico and Blake and the rest of the children walked together.

At the penguin habitat, all the tension about cameras and contests disappeared when the children saw how cute the babies were.

"Oooh," Violet gushed. She waited until Benny had taken the first picture before asking if she could take one, too. He handed her the camera.

Jessie pulled out her notebook. She jotted down a few of the facts Mr. Newton was telling them about the babies.

"Penguins babies live in rookeries, or groups, where they all huddle together to stay warm," Mr. Newton told the group. He pointed to a baby huddled next to some adults. "They also have soft feathers called down to help protect them from the cold."

Blake snapped a picture of the baby penguins.

While Mr. Newton talked, Jessie noticed that Sophie was growing more and more sad and quiet.

"Are you okay?" Jessie asked Sophie.

Sophie bit her bottom lip. "I guess so," she replied. "The baby penguins are just so adorable. I'm not sure I'll be able to remember how great they are once we leave here. Sometimes I wish my parents had a little extra money for things other than swimming. Like cameras."

Jessie put her arm around Sophie. "But just think, you're the only one here who has a chance at making it to the Olympics. That's a once-in-a-lifetime thing."

Jessie's words seemed to make Sophie feel a little better. "I guess there will always be baby animals to take pictures of, right?"

"Exactly," Jessie told her. "New babies are born at the zoo every year!"

At that, Sophie smiled and headed off after Benny and Mr. Newton toward the giraffe habitat.

Once they all got there, Henry and Violet stood at the fence looking at the newest little giraffe.

"The baby's so wobbly on those toothpick legs," Henry said to Violet. "It's amazing that he can stand up at all."

Blake squeezed in between Violet and Henry, shoving his way toward the fence. "Excuse me," he said. "This is the best spot for a contest-winning picture." Violet took a step back.

Henry tried to move to let Blake get right up next to the fence, but Annika was shoving her way in on his other side. Henry was sandwiched between the two photographers.

"I saw this spot first!" Annika said, putting the camera to her eye to frame the picture.

"It doesn't matter." Blake put his camera up to his eye, too. "I have the better angle."

"Looks to me like they are taking the same shot," Violet commented to Jessie.

"Sure does. It's the same view. Same position. Same baby giraffe," Jessie said.

Blake and Annika clicked their camera buttons at the exact same time.

"Done!" Blake said, stepping back from the fence.

"Whew," Henry said, finally able to breathe. "I'm surprised you don't want to take a few more pictures to make sure you got it just right."

"When you have a winning photo, all it takes is one shot," Blake said with certainty. He glanced over at Annika, who was busy taking multiple shots of the same view. "I think I'll use this camera, with the winning picture, for the rest of today. Then I'll have a completely new one to use tomorrow." Blake patted his over-the-shoulder bag.

Annika leaned over to the fence and clicked her tongue. "Come here, little giraffe," she said. She fired off another couple of pictures.

"Henry," Benny said, rushing up to the others. "Have you seen Sophie?"

Henry looked around the group. "No. Why?"

"I don't see her," said Benny. "Being an assistant zoologist is hard work. It's my first day, and I already lost a tourist."

"Sophie's not lost," Violet said. She pointed to the tall blond girl sitting alone by the nearby picnic area. "There she is."

Sophie was far off from the group. She was sitting in the grass. Instead of looking at the giraffes, she watched some peacocks.

"I'll go get her," Benny said.

Benny scampered off and came back a minute later without Sophie. "She says giraffes are boring," he told the others. "She's waiting for us to get done with the giraffes so we can eat lunch."

"Let's go, then," Blake said, holding his bag tightly against his chest. "I'm hungry."

Benny rubbed his tummy. "I've been so busy today, I forgot to eat my snacks. I'm starving!"

Everyone went over to the picnic tables, where Sophie joined them.

The lunch cooler was there, waiting for them. The students set their cameras and backpacks on a table and went to get their lunch sacks.

For a few minutes, Nico was alone at the table. Then Benny came rushing over. "Here. These are for you." Benny gave Nico an orange, a bottle of water, and some chips from his pack.

Sophie, Blake, Annika, and the twins sat on one side of the table, with Nico and the Aldens on the other. The rest of the tour group sat with Mr. Newton at another table.

"I'm not very hungry," Henry said. He gave Nico half of his turkey sandwich, too.

"You Aldens are lifesavers!" Nico said, perking up after taking a bite of Henry's sandwich. "Thanks a million!"

A few bites into lunch, a fight broke out at the far end of the picnic table.

"I want to take a picture of that bird," said Griffin. He was pointing at a peacock pen near the lunch tables.

"You can't," his twin Matthew said. "You took the last three pictures. It's my turn. And I don't like peacocks."

"But he's a pretty bird," Griffin said. "And his feathers are all spread out. Quick. Give me the camera."

Matthew hid it behind his back. "No way," he said.

Griffin reached over and pushed his twin, so Matthew shoved back. "If you want to take so many pictures, get your own camera," Matthew said.

"Fine! I will get my own camera." Griffin stood up and grabbed his lunch bag. Then he went and sat with the rest of the group at the other table.

"Tour group!" Mr. Newton called. He rushed up to the tables. "Some new butterflies are hatching from their cocoons!" Mr. Newton excitedly announced. "Let's head over to the butterfly pavilion right now. The ones that hatched a few days ago are taking flight for the first time!"

The children from the tour quickly started to clean up.

Annika grabbed her camera off the table, stuffed her half-eaten food back into its sack, then walked over and dumped it in the cooler.

Blake was about to head over to the cooler, but he picked up his camera first. "I'd better put this away before anything bad happens to it," he said. He shoved the camera into his over-the-shoulder bag and laid the bag on the table. Then Blake went over to the cooler with his leftover lunch.

The rest of the spring break tour group rushed about, gathering their cameras and lunches. They were in a hurry to see the butterflies.

On their way, a zookeeper and a woman wearing a security badge walked by. They were carrying a small monkey in a metal cage. It jumped about and made hooting sounds.

"I can't wait to get to the monkey area," Violet said.

"I think we're seeing them at the end of the day," Henry told her.

They finally entered the butterfly pavilion. "This is incredible," Jessie said.

There were butterflies all around, on branches and bushes. One even landed for an instant on Benny's head. Violet quickly took a picture before it flew away.

Mr. Newton told the children that once the butterflies come out of their cocoons, they need to hang upside-down for a while

so their wings can expand and dry before they fly. Some of the butterflies were just coming out. Others, like the one that landed on Benny's head, had emerged a few days earlier.

When the tour group left the butterfly pavilion, the students went on to see some newly hatched hummingbirds. They were resting in their cup-shaped nest, waiting for their mother to return and feed them. After that, the group followed Mr. Newton and Benny to the baby alligators' habitat. When they arrived, the small alligators were sunning themselves on rocks to keep warm. Henry took a few pictures.

At the jaguar exhibit, it was Jessie's turn with the Alden camera. She focused on a baby jaguar, climbing up a tree. But she was suddenly interrupted by Blake shouting. "My camera! It's gone! Someone stole my camera!" he said.

CHAPTER 3

A Mystery

Mr. Newton rushed over to Blake and confirmed that Blake only had one of his two cameras. He then called the group together. "We have a problem," Mr. Newton announced. "Blake's camera is missing. If you have a camera, please check and make sure that it is yours."

"How would we know if it is Blake's camera?" asked Matthew. He looked at the camera in his hand. "I think this is mine and Griffin's, but it doesn't have our names on it."

"Yes. All the cameras we bought this morning look alike," Griffin added. "They're twins, just like me and my brother!" The twins high-fived each other. It seemed like they were back to being friends.

"Is there any chance *you* put *your* name on it?" Henry asked Blake.

"I didn't think I had to," Blake said. He was growing angry. "Someone *took* it. They knew my best picture was on that camera so they stole it!" He looked around at the group, staring at each person there. "Who did it?" Blake asked. "Who has my camera?"

"Slow down," Jessie said to Blake. "Maybe someone took it, but it also might have fallen out of your bag. It's always best to look around before accusing people of stealing."

"We'll help you find it," Benny said. "The Aldens are good at solving mysteries."

"Can you remember where you saw the camera last?" Violet asked as Jessie pulled her notebook out of her backpack pocket.

"It was in here." Blake dumped everything out of his bag onto a bench.

"A pen, the zoo ticket, a bottle of water, a pack of gum, and a camera," Jessie said, looking through the things from Blake's bag. "No second camera."

Violet picked up the camera. "How do you know the missing one had the giraffe photo on it?"

Blake pointed to the top. There was a little dial that showed how many pictures had been taken. "Zero," he read. "I didn't take any pictures with this camera yet. I was saving it for tomorrow."

"When did you last use the missing camera?" Henry asked.

"I haven't seen anything I wanted to take pictures of since before lunch," Blake said, trying to recall. As he thought, Blake rubbed a hand over his red hair. "So the last time I used it must have been at the giraffe exhibit."

"Okay," Henry said. "We need to retrace our steps and go back to the places we've visited today."

Blake glared at Annika as if she was guilty. "You knew I had a great photo on that camera. You wanted me to lose the contest, didn't you?" He squinted at her. "I bet you took it."

"I didn't take your camera," Annika replied. "I only have this one." She held up her camera.

Mr. Newton began to break the students into small groups. "Jessie and Violet will go with Sophie and Nico back to the giraffe exhibit." He pointed in the direction of the giraffes.

"I'll go with Benny and Blake to the butterflies," Henry suggested. "That was our first stop after lunch."

"I'll go with you, Henry," Annika said. "Even though Blake accused me of being a thief, I'll still help look around." Annika huffed. "I'll prove I am innocent."

"Fine. That's the second group. Blake, Henry, Benny, and Annika," said Mr. Newton.

"Where do we go?" the Cho twins asked at the same time.

"You two can come along with me," Mr.

Newton said. He gathered everyone else into his group, too. Then he took the flag from Benny. "My team is heading back to the hummingbirds and then to the alligators." Mr. Newton checked his watch. "We are going to meet in half an hour under the big banner announcing the baby monkeys." He pointed at a nearby sign with a picture of little monkeys hanging from a tree. "It's not very far from here. If you don't see me, look for the flag."

Mr. Newton wished the students good luck, and everyone went on their separate ways.

"Come on," Henry told Blake and his group. They began to head off to the butterfly pavilion. "We're going to find that camera."

"I hope so," Blake said. "But I'm sure we won't. I know it was stolen."

* * *

"How do we get to the giraffes?" Violet asked Jessie as they headed in a different direction.

Pushing his shaggy hair out of his eyes, Nico looked closely at the sign that Mr. Newton had shown them. "That way is the monkeys," he said. "I see the signs for hippos and elephants. But there isn't a picture of giraffes."

"Forget it," Sophie said. "Let's skip the giraffes. There's no way that Blake lost the camera there. It would be a huge waste of time to walk all the way back to the giraffes."

"We told Mr. Newton and Henry we'd go to the giraffes. We better do what we said." Jessie hurried over to a man in a zoo uniform selling balloons and asked for directions.

The man took a map out of his pocket. He said, "We are here." He pointed to the jaguar exhibit. "You need to head that way."

"Okay, thanks," Jessie said, taking the map from the man. "Let's hurry. We only have half an hour."

Nico took off toward the giraffes, saying, "Long-neck friends, here we come!"

Nico got there first. Jessie and Violet were right behind him. They started looking around for the camera. But moments later, Jessie realized that Sophie wasn't with them.

"Oh no," Jessie said. "Not again. This is just like when Benny thought she was missing the last time we were here."

Jessie and Violet stopped looking for the camera and searched for Sophie instead. They searched for a tall girl with blond hair in the zoo crowds, but couldn't find her.

Giving up for the moment, they went to get Nico instead.

"I can't find the camera anywhere," Nico told the girls the instant they approached. "I even looked down there." He pointed over the fence to where the baby giraffe was eating leaves from a low bush. "But there's no camera on the ground of the habitat."

"No camera," Jessie said. "And, no Sophie either."

"What do you mean?" Nico asked, peering over Jessie's shoulder. "She's behind you."

Jessie swung her head around. Sophie was a little ways back from the giraffe cage, close to where they'd stopped to eat lunch.

"What? How?" Violet was confused. "I am sure she wasn't over there a second ago."

Jessie walked over to the picnic area. "Where were you?" she asked.

Sophie pointed at the tables. "I was checking the lunch area." She looked at Nico. "Any luck?"

"Nah," Nico said. "You?"

"Nope," Sophie said, glancing over at the giraffes with a shiver. "Let's get out of here."

As they walked away, Jessie put her hand on Violet's arm, a silent sign to hang back. Jessie was still holding her notebook in her hand. "I think if no one finds the camera, Sophie should be our first suspect."

"I thought we weren't accusing anyone yet," Violet said to her sister.

"I'm just thinking," Jessie said. She then jotted down Sophie's name in her book. "Sophie didn't want to look for the camera, and then, once we got here, she disappeared. Maybe she doesn't want to look because she's the one who took it."

"Why would Sophie take it?" Violet asked.

"She wanted a camera and couldn't afford one, right?" Jessie answered.

"But if she suddenly had a new camera this afternoon, everyone would know it wasn't hers," Violet said.

"You're right," Jessie said. "But, she's acting so strangely, it makes me wonder what's going on."

Violet pressed her lips together, considering Jessie's words. "She does keep on disappearing. Hmmm." Violet paused. "Okay," she said at last. "If no one finds the camera by the time we all meet at the monkeys, Sophie Webb will be suspect number one in Blake's missing camera mystery."

CHAPTER 4

Monkey Trouble

Benny, Henry, Annika, and Blake didn't find the camera at the butterfly exhibit, so they hurried on to catch up with the rest of the group.

"There! That's where we're supposed to meet Mr. Newton." Benny rushed up to a cage where little monkeys were swinging from trees and playing with ropes. "Those are the baby monkeys."

"Where is the banner that Mr. Newton mentioned?" Henry looked all around. "I don't see him or the rest of the group."

Pushing through a crowd of tourists, Henry looked closely at the monkeys. "Those aren't babies," Henry told Benny. "They are capuchins. From—" He leaned in to see the sign. "—South America. It says here that the average capuchin weighs no more than six pounds."

"They're not babies?" Benny asked. "Hmm. They sure look like babies to me."

"Figures," Blake said, pressing in next to Henry and Benny. "We're in the wrong place."

"But we can't be far," Benny told him. "This whole area is full of monkeys. We just need to find the baby ones. Ack!" Benny jumped back, surprised, when one of the little capuchins swung onto a branch right in front of him. "Oooh, oooh!" the monkey squawked at him.

"He's trying to play with you," Henry told Benny.

The little monkey pointed at Benny's backpack.

"You want my snacks, don't you?" Benny asked. "Sorry. I'm just an assistant zoologist, so I don't know what monkeys eat. And I only have people food in my pack." Benny waved at the monkey.

The monkey waved back, then pointed at Benny's pack again.

It was like a game. The monkey would point and Benny would wave, and the monkey always waved back.

Finally, Blake said, "We better find the rest of the group. It's already been half an hour."

"When we find them, I hope they have your camera," Annika added, shaking her head. "I really wish we'd found it." She looked at Blake. "Stop staring at me," she said. "I can tell you still think I took it."

"Well, who else would it be?" Blake asked her. "Do you think Benny took it?"

"Me?" Benny asked, eyes wide. "I didn't steal any cameras!"

His red hair glittered in the sunlight as Blake gave a little smile. "I know. You had no reason to steal it. The only person who had a reason is Annika."

At that, Annika turned and dumped her purse onto a nearby bench. She emptied her coat pockets. She even turned her jeans pockets inside out. "See?!" she told Blake. "No camera except this one." She held up her camera. "Mine. Not yours."

"I still think—" Blake started, but Henry cut him off.

"Maybe one of the other groups found your camera, Blake," Henry said.

"Let's try going this way." Benny pointed around the back of the capuchin cage. "See ya," he told his new little friend.

And just then, the little monkey fiddled with the cage door. To everyone's surprise, the door opened.

The next thing Benny knew, the monkey was sitting on his shoulder, trying to get into Benny's pack.

"Oh no!" Benny said, trying to pull his pack away. "Help! A monkey broke out of his cage!"

"Hold still," a voice echoed through the

crowd. A zookeeper had been feeding the chimpanzees their lunch in a cage across the way. He heard Benny's call for help. "I'm on my way," the zookeeper called.

A tourist holding an ice cream cone was surprised as the little capuchin leapt off Benny's backpack and made a grab for his dessert. "Get away!" the man shouted.

The man's wife waved her arms wildly to chase the monkey away. "Don't let the monkey near any children!" she cried.

The monkey gave up on the ice cream cone and jumped through the crowd.

In the short minute it took for the zookeeper to arrive, the little monkey had stolen a pretzel from a girl and an apple from a boy in a stroller.

The little boy's mother started yelling. "Help! The monkey's after my kids!"

The monkey dashed around. The zookeeper was now after him, shouting to the people in the crowd, "Don't panic. Simio is not dangerous. Stay still and I'll catch him."

"There you are!" Mr. Newton came up

to where Henry, Annika, Blake, and Benny were standing, watching the zookeeper chase the monkey. The rest of the tour group was with him.

"What is going on?!" Mr. Newton said. He shoved his glasses back up his nose and looked around. "Seems like we have monkey trouble. I can't believe Simio escaped *again*. Zookeeper Frank told me that they found him over by the butterflies earlier today. We keep changing the cage door lock, but he opens it every time. Simio is a clever capuchin."

"And a hungry monkey, too," Benny said. He watched Simio take a bite of a little girl's cotton candy. The monkey now wore a pink fuzzy beard.

"Maybe you should change his name to Houdini," Henry suggested.

"Who-di-ni?" Benny asked.

"Harry Houdini was a famous escape artist and magician," Jessie told him. "He could get out of any cage."

"Funny," Mr. Newton said with a small

laugh. "That's definitely a more fitting name than Simio. *Simio* is a scientific name for monkeys in Spanish." Then Mr. Newton heard a shout behind him. "I better go help Zookeeper Frank," he said.

Zookeeper Frank had Simio cornered by a rock. The zookeeper reached forward, but like lightning, Simio jumped up and scampered away. Frustrated, Zookeeper Frank told Mr. Newton to call the security office. "We need a tranquilizer gun," he said.

"Oh no! You can't shoot him," Violet put her hands on her cheeks. "That would be terrible. Monkeys are my favorite! I don't want to see one hurt!"

"It's not so bad, Violet," Henry said to his sister. "They'll shoot him with a dart that has medicine on the tip. It'll make Simio go to sleep. Once he's sleeping, they can carry him back to his cage."

"I don't like that plan," Violet said, shaking her head. "There must be something else we can do!"

They rushed over to Zookeeper Frank and

Mr. Newton. All the other kids in the tour group followed them. When they got close, the children heard a woman's voice over Mr. Newton's walkie-talkie speaker. "Security," a woman answered. "What's the situation?"

While Mr. Newton explained to the security officer what was going on at the monkey habitat, Benny pulled off his backpack and set it down. "Zookeeper Frank? Do capuchins like fruit?"

"Yes, they do. Capuchin monkeys eat a lot of fruit. They also eat nuts, seeds, and even insects," the zookeeper answered.

Benny pulled an apple out of his pack. He gave an orange to Henry and Jessie. Then passed a banana to Violet. "Maybe Simio will follow a fruit trail to his cage?"

"Great idea!" Zookeeper Frank told Benny. "If we can get him back into the cage, then we won't have to tranquilize him." He agreed to help the Alden children try their plan.

Henry unpeeled the orange and took a bite. He let the juice drip a little on his chin. "Yummmm," he said in a clear, loud voice.

Jessie stepped closer to the cage. She opened her orange, too, and waved part of the peel. "Come and get it," she said.

The monkey glanced from Henry to Jessie and back again. Then, slowly, very slowly, he stepped forward. Just a little.

"I'll open the cage," Zookeeper Frank told Benny in a whispered voice. When the door was open, he told Benny to stand next to the entry. Zookeeper Frank blocked the door so none of the other monkeys in the habitat could escape. They were all high up in the trees, swinging from limb to limb.

Simio took a bite of the orange Henry held in his hand and then jumped over the heads of Griffin and Matthew to where Jessie stood. Griffin took a quick photo of the little monkey.

"If he gets a hold of the orange, he'll jump into a tree to eat it," Zookeeper Frank told the children. "Don't let him have the whole thing."

Simio licked at the orange tightly held in Jessie's hand. "He likes it," she whispered.

Violet stood a little closer to the cage door, eating a bite of banana.

Bored with Jessie's orange, Simio leapt toward Violet. His sudden move surprised her, and she very nearly dropped the banana.

"Just hold tight," Zookeeper Frank told her. "Simio might be very energetic, but he's also very friendly."

Violet held out the banana as far as her arm could stretch.

One bite of the warm yellow fruit, and Simio was off again. He returned to Jessie's orange.

"Wrong way!" Benny told the monkey. "Come get the apple."

It was as if the monkey understood what Benny had said.

Simio took one more nibble on Jessie's orange. Then he jumped through the crowd. He went back over the twins, passing by Violet and her banana. Finally, the monkey dashed right up to Benny and put out two paws, asking for the red fruit in Benny's hand.

Benny pointed to a tree branch inside the

cage. "Go sit on that branch. I'll give you the apple."

Simio leapt past Benny and sat down on the tree branch inside the cage, just like Benny had told him to.

"Yippee!" Jessie and Violet shouted.

Benny gave Simio the apple, then jumped out of the capuchin habitat. Zookeeper Frank immediately shut the door behind him. When the security team showed up with the dart gun, Benny said proudly, "The monkey emergency is already fixed!"

"Now, I'm going to figure out a way to fix this lock for good," Zookeeper Frank announced. "Simio has had enough adventures!"

Mr. Newton came rushing forward. "You are an excellent assistant zoologist!" he said to Benny. Then he gave Benny a high-five.

Benny was smiling. "This is the most exciting job I've ever had," he told Mr. Newton.

Mr. Newton led the group back to the red Educational Center barn. "It's nearly three o'clock," he told them. "Our first day of touring is over. When you come back tomorrow, I'll make sure we see the baby monkeys and the rest of the newborn animals. Don't forget your cameras," he added. "And if you didn't buy one today, you can bring five dollars tomorrow."

"But what about my missing camera?" Blake asked.

In the confusion of the monkey escape, no one had reported if they'd found it or not.

Shoving his glasses up on his nose once again, Mr. Newton sighed. "We didn't find it," he said. "I'm so sorry."

"I knew it! My camera was stolen." Blake moved away from Mr. Newton and marched up to Henry, Jessie, Violet, and Benny. He pointed toward the lunch cooler where Sophie and Annika were collecting their bags. "I think Annika should be the number one suspect!"

CHAPTER 5

Suspects and Clues

"Blake still may have lost the camera," Henry said to his sisters. He laid his head all the way back on his beanbag chair, looking up at the boxcar clubhouse ceiling. "We might not have searched hard enough. Or maybe someone picked it up. Did anyone check the zoo's lost-and-found?"

Jessie typed a note into her computer. "Let's do that first thing tomorrow."

"In case we don't find it, it'll be good to get a list of suspects ready," Violet said. "That way, we'll know who to keep an eye on while we finish the zoo babies tour. Maybe one of us will see something suspicious."

"Like when we thought Sophie was acting suspicious?" Jessie asked, typing *Sophie Webb* under a heading that said: *Suspects.*

"Exactly," Violet agreed.

Henry sat up a little. "Suspicious?" he asked. "Tell me what you saw." But before the girls could answer, Benny came bounding into the clubhouse. He was carrying a big bowl of popcorn. Watch, the Alden children's dog, was right behind him.

"Snack time!" he announced, setting the bowl on a small table and dragging his own beanbag chair over. Watch lay down on the floor.

"We just had dinner," Jessie said.

"Eating popcorn is like eating air," Benny told his sister. "It takes up no room in your tummy." He patted his belly before stuffing a handful of the treat into his mouth. "Mmmm."

Violet took a few kernels before turning to

Henry and answering his question. "Sophie disappeared at the giraffe cage when we were seeing the babies."

"And then," Jessie went on, "she stayed away from the giraffes when we went back there the second time."

"That is odd," Henry said. "But it doesn't make her a thief."

"I still think we should ask Sophie about the giraffes," Violet told Jessie. "Write that down, okay?"

"Got it." Jessie saved the document, then scrolled down the page. "Sophie is our first suspect. Who should be next?"

"Blake said he wanted Annika to be suspect number one," Benny said. "See? I'm a good witness and a good rememberer, too." He grinned.

"Show-off," said Henry, laughing. He took a single piece of popcorn and tossed it at Benny playfully. Benny caught it and gobbled it down.

"Are there any clues that lead to her?" Jessie asked.

"Only that she and Blake both want to win the contest," Henry said.

"She didn't want Blake to have two cameras," Violet added. "He could be right. She might have taken one to make things more fair."

"Or to win their deal that I was the witness for!" Benny said. "But Annika keeps telling Blake she's innocent."

"But isn't that what all thieves do?" Violet asked. "Say they are innocent?"

"Hmm." Henry rubbed his chin, thinking. "It's also what innocent people say."

"I'll put her down as suspect number two for now," Jessie said, typing.

"Who else?" Violet looked at her brothers and sister.

"Well," Henry said after a quiet pause. "There's Nico. He really wished he had a camera. And he was all alone at the picnic table at lunch when everybody's stuff was on the table. Maybe he took Blake's camera then. I guess we'll know whether or not he took Blake's camera if he has his own camera tomorrow and he doesn't buy one from Mr. Newton."

"We need to watch everyone coming in tomorrow morning," Jessie said. "Some kids will buy new cameras. But we have to be on the lookout for anyone who might have a zoo camera but did not buy it."

Benny petted Watch's head and thought for a moment. "I am Mr. Newton's assistant zoologist," he said. "I helped him sell the cameras today. Tomorrow, I'll be able to help again and make sure everyone who has a camera paid for it." Then he added, "This has been a very exciting spring break. Maybe the most exciting one ever."

"It certainly has been interesting," Henry agreed. Turning to Jessie he asked, "So we have three suspects, right?"

"We can add one more," Jessie said. "I think Griffin should be on our list." She typed his name down. "He and Matthew got into that big fight at lunch over the camera they were sharing," she explained.

"So you think one of them took Blake's

camera?" Henry asked her. "Why Griffin and not Matthew?"

"Well," Jessie said, "he was the one who stomped off without a camera saying he'd get himself one."

"Oh!" Violet said, figuring out what her sister was thinking. "But when Simio was running around loose, it was Griffin who took the picture! Where'd he get the camera?"

"That's right," Henry said. "I remember thinking that a picture of the monkey might be a good one for the contest. But I was helping with the fruit trap. Okay, then, Griffin is suspect number four."

Benny finished the last little bit of popcorn. "I need a drink," he said, standing and picking up the bowl. "All that popped air made me thirsty!"

"Are we done for tonight?" Violet asked.

Jessie nodded yes. She printed out the suspects page and taped it into her notebook, ready for the next day at the zoo. "I could use a drink, too," she added.

"Hot chocolate?" Henry suggested.

"Yum!" Jessie said, turning off the lights in the boxcar. "And then to bed!" She gave Benny a kiss on his head. "We all need a good night's sleep. Tomorrow, we are going to find Blake's camera."

* * *

When they arrived at the zoo the next morning, Violet and Henry put all the Alden lunch bags in the cooler. Meanwhile, Jessie and Benny got permission to go to the main office to check the lost-and-found.

Benny dug deep through a cardboard box filled with lost items. There were sweaters and hats and other things the zookeepers had found after the zoo closed.

"Here's a tennis shoe!" Benny said, reaching to the bottom of the collection. "How do you think someone lost a shoe? Did they wear only one home?"

"That's an interesting mystery for another time," Jessie said with a laugh. "Any cameras?"

Benny sorted through everything. "Nope," he said. "But wait a second." Benny leaned so far over the side of the box that his feet came off the floor. He rummaged around for a minute, but then he couldn't get out on his own. "Pull me out, Jessie. I'm stuck," he said.

Jessie grabbed Benny's feet and tugged. He tumbled out of the box holding a bracelet. It was a silver link chain with a charm on it.

"What's that charm?" Jesse asked, looking carefully at the bracelet. "Why, it's a tiny swimmer, isn't it?" She flipped the charm over. There was an *S* engraved on the back.

"I think it might be Sophie's," Benny said. He took a closer look. "But she didn't say anything about losing a bracelet yesterday."

Jessie nodded at Benny, then turned and asked a nearby attendant if it was okay to take the bracelet. "We think we know who this belongs to," Jessie told the woman.

"Please bring it back if you can't find the owner," the woman said.

Jessie agreed and tucked the bracelet into her pocket.

"We better get back to the group," Jessie told Benny. "We have questions to ask Sophie Webb."

The two of them hurried back to the Educational Center's red barn.

Mr. Newton was already selling cameras.

"Oh no," Benny said. "Some kids have new cameras, but I didn't see them pay."

Benny pointed at Griffin, who was snapping pictures around the barn. "Like Griffin. How do I know if he just bought that one or if it's Blake's?"

"Let's hope that Henry and Violet saw who stood in line," Jessie said.

Jessie hurried over to Violet. She was standing with Nico. Jessie almost didn't recognize him. Nico had his shaggy hair tucked under a baseball cap.

"Did you see who bought cameras?" Jessie whispered to her sister.

"No," Violet admitted. "We were early, but other kids were even earlier! When we showed up, Mr. Newton had already started selling cameras. We saw Griffin and a few others buy cameras. But mostly . . . we missed it."

"Hmm," Jessie said. "I'm not sure how

we're going to solve this mystery now."

"It was too easy thinking that we could just watch for who has a camera but didn't buy one," Henry said, coming over to the girls. "Mysteries are never that easy."

"It might be a little harder to figure out, but we're very good detectives!" Violet said.

Jessie noticed that Nico had a camera now. He was busy writing his name on it in pen. "After what happened yesterday with Blake," he was saying, "I'm not taking any chances. This is *my* camera."

"Did you just buy that?" Jessie asked Nico.

"Yes," he said, handing the pen to Sophie.

Then Jessie saw that Sophie had a camera, too. *But just yesterday she said her parents wouldn't let her get one*, Jesse thought.

"Did you just buy that?" Jessie asked, pointing to Sophie's camera.

"It's mine," Sophie said, writing her name on the camera.

Henry pulled Jessie aside. Benny followed them. "Asking everyone if they bought a camera is not going to work," Henry said.

"If someone stole Blake's camera, he or she might lie about whether or not they bought one."

Jessie shrugged. "I was hoping someone would just confess." She took out her notebook. Flipping it open, she turned to where she had taped the printed suspects list they had typed up the night before. "I suppose we should go ahead and interview the suspects like we planned."

"That's right, Jessie," Benny said. "We have more questions for Sophie."

Jessie agreed and pulled the bracelet out of her pocket. She led Benny back over to Sophie. "Is this yours?" Jessie asked. She held out the little charm bracelet for Sophie to see.

"Yes! Thank you!" Sophie took the bracelet. "Where'd you find it?"

"In the lost-and-found," Benny said.

"Well, I am so glad. I didn't know how I was going to explain to my parents that it was missing. They spent a lot to get it for my last birthday." Sophie clasped the bracelet around her wrist and began to move over to the chair area.

"Wait, Sophie," Violet said. "Yesterday I noticed that you stayed far away from the giraffes. Is there a reason?"

Sophie stopped and shuddered. A shiver went all the way through her. "I don't like giraffes."

"You don't like them?" Jessie asked. "Really?"

"Ugh," Sophie said. "When I was little, my parents bought me a stuffed giraffe toy. At night, in the dark, it looked so creepy with that long, long neck! I used to have bad dreams about giraffes. My parents finally had to take the toy away and give it to another kid." She wrapped her arms around herself and said, "I know it's silly, but those things still scare me!"

"That explains everything!" Benny said.

"What?" Sophie asked.

"Why you acted strange and disappeared at the giraffe's habitat," he told her. "We thought it might be because you took the camera and didn't want to go back to the scene of the crime."

"That's what you thought?" Sophie said with a small laugh. "I just didn't want to go see the giraffes." She shook her head and walked away. "I can't believe you thought I was the thief," she muttered.

Jessie took out her notebook. "Sophie isn't a suspect anymore. She said that the camera was hers, and I think I believe her. Sophie also explained that she acted weird yesterday because she was scared." With her pen, Jessie drew a line though Sophie's name. "One down, three to go. Annika's next."

CHAPTER 6

More Monkey Madness

The instant he entered the room, Blake went running up to the Aldens. "Did you solve the mystery?" he asked, out of breath. "Did you find my missing camera?" Blake's red hair was sticking up, as if he'd tossed and turned all night. His eyes looked dark, too. It was obvious Blake hadn't slept well the night before.

"Not yet," Henry told Blake. "But we're narrowing down our suspects."

"Have you interviewed Annika?" Blake asked.

"We're about to do that now," Jessie told him.

"Good," Blake said. "Tell her to give me back my camera."

"If we find out that she took it, we'll let you know," Violet said.

Benny was supposed to interview Annika, but Mr. Newton called him to the front. Mr. Newton was carrying a heavy animal cage. He set it down on the floor at the front of the room.

"I better go," Benny told Violet. "I didn't get here in time to help with all the cameras. Mr. Newton's counting on me to be his assistant zoologist again today. And I want to do a good job!"

Benny smiled, then rubbed his tummy. "If I do a good job, I get to go first at tonight's pizza party. Mr. Newton promised! So can we interview Annika while we walk around the zoo?"

"Of course," Violet said, and Benny rushed off. Then she turned to Jessie. "I think you can go ahead and cross Griffin off the suspect list. He bought a camera this morning. He's one of the few I saw buy one."

"But yesterday, he took a picture of the monkey," Henry said. "Whose camera was that?"

"He and Matthew were friends again by then," Violet said. "Now that I think about it, they high-fived each other by the jaguar habitat. And that was after Blake announced that his camera was missing. I guess Griffin was back to sharing with his brother."

"Okay," Jessie scratched out his name. "What about Nico?"

"He's still a suspect," Violet said. "He has a camera, but none of us saw him buy it."

Henry had an idea. He rushed over to where Mr. Newton was busy getting a little monkey out of the cage. Benny was helping, holding the end of a red leather leash.

"Is that Simio?" Henry asked, momentarily distracted from what he meant to ask.

"It sure is!" Mr. Newton said. "Simio might not be a baby monkey, but we can still learn a lot from him."

"Great!" Henry was excited and turned to go to his sisters. "Oh," he spun back. "I almost forgot. Did you sell Nico a camera today?"

"Yes," Mr. Newton said as Simio jumped onto his shoulder. "Why?"

"Just checking," Henry said.

Then Henry went back to his sisters, eager to sit down and learn about the monkey.

"Nico's in the clear," he told his sisters. "He bought the camera this morning."

"Did you ask about Sophie, too?" Jessie asked her brother.

"No," he said. "I thought we decided she wasn't a suspect anymore."

"I still wonder . . . " Jessie looked at Sophie's name in the notebook. She reread the clues that pointed to her and checked each one off. "Forget it," Jessie said at last. "I think she's innocent. After the monkey show, we'll talk to Annika. She must have taken the camera. There's no one else on our list."

"She had the biggest reason to take it," Henry said.

Jessie looked over at Annika. She was taking pictures of Mr. Newton and the monkey.

"Hey!" Annika suddenly shouted. "That's mine."

Jessie, Henry, and Violet all rushed over to see what happened.

"Give it back!" Annika told Simio.

Simio had reached backward from his perch on Mr. Newton's shoulder. He grabbed the camera right out of Annika's hands!

She put out her palm. "Not funny," Annika told the monkey. "Give it back. Now."

Simio hooted at her and held it up too high for her to reach.

Mr. Newton swung the monkey off his shoulder. "Come on, Simio," he said gently. "That isn't yours." He took the camera easily out of Simio's hands and gave it back to Annika.

At first, Annika looked surprised that is was so easy for Mr. Newton to take the camera back. "Thanks little guy!" Annika said. Then she took another picture of Simio before she went and sat down.

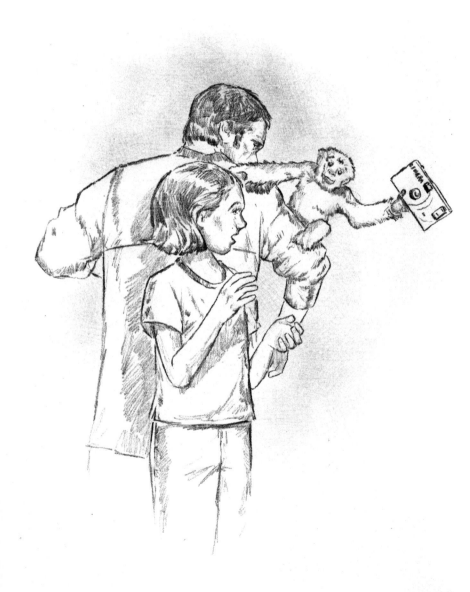

Mr. Newton smiled after her, then cleared his throat. "Students, everyone, please sit down," he said. "I want to teach you what this terrific little monkey can do."

He set Simio on the ground in the center of the circle and told Benny to remove the leash.

"Are you sure?" Benny asked, eyes wide. "He could escape again."

"That's an interesting thought, Benny," Mr. Newton said. "But Simio's only good at picking cage locks. The doors here have a different kind of lock, so I'm not worried about him getting loose. I want to show you the great tricks he knows."

After Benny took off Simio's leash, Mr. Newton held up a hoop for Simio. The monkey jumped through it and everyone applauded. He gave Simio a jump rope, and the monkey skipped rope a few times. Then, he placed a large ball on the floor in front of Simio. Simio looked at it.

"Toss it to me," Mr. Newton told him. Simio stared at the ball, and then, instead of tossing it, he leapt over it and ran over to Annika. He snagged the camera right out of her hands. Again.

Then, Simio ran around the room, randomly grabbing various items from the students. Before anyone could stop him, the monkey had made a big pile of cameras, jackets, water bottles, and other items in the center of the room. He even took Mr. Newton's glasses!

Mr. Newton kept calling his name. "Simio. Stop!" But Simio was happily running around, squawking and collecting.

"Add monkeys to the list of animals I don't like," Sophie said as Simio quickly hopped by. "I'm scared of monkeys now, too. I'm going to have nightmares tonight about a monkey stealing my stuff."

Mr. Newton grabbed at the little fellow, but Simio was fast. "Benny, I need your help," he said. "Let's use your fruit trick again. We have to get him back in the cage."

"I'll get my backpack," Benny said, hurrying to the back of the room.

He reached into his bag, which was once again filled with snacks. "Here!" said Benny as he tossed Henry an orange. Just like he had done the day before, Henry peeled the fruit and offered it to Simio. But the monkey was busy stealing another water bottle.

"It isn't working," Henry told Benny.

"Just wait," Benny said. "If his tummy is anything like mine, he won't be able to stay away from good food."

And sure enough, after tossing the container onto his pile of things, Simio came back for a bite of the fruit.

Mr. Newton caught Simio this time while Henry was feeding him the orange.

"You have a smart tummy," Henry told Benny while Mr. Newton put the little monkey back in the carrying cage.

"Simio is always hungry. Just like me," Benny said, smiling. He peeled his own orange and bit into a segment.

"Sorry about that," Mr. Newton told the group. "Capuchin monkeys spend their days searching for food. It could be that he thought he was collecting food." Mr. Newton shrugged. "Clearly he isn't as well-trained as I thought."

"Maybe he's just excited by all the kids," Annika said as she searched the pile for her camera.

The sweatshirts and jackets were easy to identify. The water bottles were in many different colors, so the kids could tell which ones were theirs. Sophie gave Mr. Newton back his glasses. After they had picked up the most obvious things, a pile of cameras remained.

"Luckily we all put our names on the cameras today," Nico said, grabbing his. "They might have gotten switched otherwise."

"Uh-oh," Matthew said as he and Griffin stood over the last two cameras.

"We both only put our last name on our cameras. And we have each taken the same number of pictures. We don't know whose is whose. What if Matthew wins the photo contest using my pictures?" Griffin picked up the two cameras and stared at them as if he might be able to tell them apart.

"Don't worry," Mr. Newton told the twins. "When I develop the film later, we can easily figure out who owns which camera by the pictures. Each of you take one now, and we can sort out the photos tonight."

The boys liked that plan and each took a camera.

When they had finally sorted out all of the things Simio had stolen, Mr. Newton went to give Benny the tour leader's flag. "Let's go see some more baby animals," Mr. Newton announced.

"You know," Henry said, "after seeing Simio steal everything in sight, it could mean that—"

"Maybe Simio took Blake's camera?!" Benny exclaimed.

"That's exactly what I was thinking," Henry said, smiling at his brother.

CHAPTER 7

Suspecting Simio

"When could Simio have taken Blake's camera?" Jessie asked Henry and Benny.

"Do you remember when we visited the butterfly pavilion after lunch yesterday?" Henry asked his sister. After she nodded, he continued. "There was a zookeeper carrying a little monkey in a cage. That might have been Simio."

"I'm sure it was! Zookeeper Frank said that the first time Simio escaped yesterday, they found him near the butterflies," Benny added.

"You really are the best rememberer ever!" Violet said, giving Benny a quick hug.

Jessie turned to Mr. Newton. "Has Simio ever escaped his cage before?"

"He's a smart monkey," Mr. Newton said with a long sigh. "Yes. He gets out all the time. Every time we change the locks, he still figures out a way to escape."

"How many times has he wandered around the zoo?" Henry asked.

"Three times that I know of," Mr. Newton said. "But I haven't been working here very long. It might be more." He gave a small smile. "Know what's funny? Even if Simio leaves the door open, none of the monkeys that share his cage ever leave. Simio's the most curious monkey we have at the zoo."

"That is funny," Benny agreed.

"Do you recall what time Simio first escaped yesterday?" Jessie asked.

"It was around lunchtime," Mr. Newton answered.

"That means that Simio really may

have been the thief! We need to search the capuchin cage for Blake's camera!" Henry exclaimed.

Mr. Newton nodded. "After his little show this morning, I think you're on the right track. Plus, I have to take Simio back to his habitat, anyway. Let's go!"

Jessie opened her notebook and looked at the suspect list she'd printed from her computer. It was still firmly taped inside. With a pencil, she added the monkey's name to the list.

The tour children all followed Mr. Newton, who was carrying Simio, to the capuchin habitat.

When they got close enough to see the habitat, Benny broke into a run. He dashed straight up to the cage door.

"I bet that camera is in there somewhere," Benny said. He stood on his tip-toes, looking into the cage through the bars.

Simio was still in the carrying cage nearby. Benny went over to him and said, "Okay, Mister. Where'd you hide it?"

The monkey scratched his head and hooted at Benny.

Benny laughed.

Mr. Newton found the correct key and opened the cage. He carried Simio inside and set him down. Then Mr. Newton closed the door, shutting them both inside the cage.

Simio climbed a tree and hung upside-down by his feet, hooting to himself.

The tour group gathered around the outside of cage. "Does anyone see the camera?" Mr. Newton asked the group.

"Maybe my camera is near those ropes." Blake shoved his nose up to the bars to get a better look at the monkey playground in the habitat.

"I don't see it," Matthew reported. "It's not over here."

Griffin was on the opposite side of the cage from his brother. "Not here, either."

"I don't see a camera anywhere," Mr. Newton said, looking around.

All of a sudden there was a loud hoot from Simio. Then there was a crashing sound.

"Ow!" said Mr. Newton. He rubbed the back of his head. "Something hit me!" His glasses had slipped down his nose. Mr. Newton pushed them back up and discovered that he had been struck by a water bottle.

"Where'd you get that?" Mr. Newton asked the monkey. Simio was hiding in a thick bush near the back of the cage. The monkey answered by throwing an apple at Mr. Newton's stomach.

This time, Mr. Newton caught it. "Nice try," he said. Mr. Newton moved closer to where the monkey was hiding. "What else do you have in there?" Mr. Newton asked. "Blake's camera maybe?"

Mr. Newton was about to reach behind the bush into Simio's hiding place when he got pelted with a bunch of animal crackers. Bits of yellow cracker got stuck in his dark hair.

"It looks like Simio is throwing all the stuff he picked up on his escape adventures around the zoo!" Matthew giggled. Then he yelled, "Mr. Newton, duck!"

Mr. Newton did, just in time, as a tennis shoe soared past his head. "Thanks for the warning," Mr. Newton told Matthew. He picked up the shoe. "That would have hurt," he added. Then he stared at the shoe a second. "Hey! Wait a minute. That's *my* shoe. It's been missing a whole week!" Mr. Newton said, looking at the monkey.

Simio hooted at Mr. Newton. Then he came out from the bushes and made a grab to get the shoe back.

"Oh, no you don't," Mr. Newton told the monkey. "What did you do with my other shoe?"

Benny grabbed Jessie's arm. "Doesn't that look like the one we found earlier in the main office?" Benny asked. Jessie nodded in agreement. "We already solved that mystery!" Benny called to Mr. Newton. "It's in the lost-and-found."

"Great work," Mr. Newton told Benny. "Now we have to find that camera!" He went around the bushes and sorted through Simio's hiding place. "A cell phone, a flip-flop, and half a sandwich. Where did you get this stuff?" he asked Simio.

"Oooh, oooh," Simio answered, jumping up and down.

"I think this monkey has escaped more times than we know," Henry told Mr. Newton.

"That explains a lot," Mr. Newton said, his head disappearing behind the bush as he finished the search. "I found the other flip-flop, but unfortunately no camera," he reported at last.

"Are you sure?" Blake asked. "It has to be there."

Mr. Newton shook his head sadly as he got up and dusted off his pants. "I'm sure," he said.

Mr. Newton addressed the students. "Okay," he said. "Enough monkey business for today. We need to give up the search. If we don't hurry, we'll never see all the new zoo babies before the spring break tour ends."

The tour group began to follow Mr. Newton on the path toward the next animal pen, where the baby gorillas lived.

Blake was disappointed. He walked up next to the Aldens and turned to Henry. "Isn't there anything more you can do?" Blake still looked very, very tired.

Henry said, "I'm not sure. Maybe we can come up with an idea."

"Annika's still a suspect, right?" Blake said hopefully.

"She's still on the list, but there really isn't any evidence that points to her," Henry told him.

"But she wants to win the contest," Blake said. "And if she wins, she'll get to be on the school newspaper staff. Aren't those reasons enough?"

"I suppose those are good reasons to keep her on the list. We'll talk to her now," Jessie said, taking out her notebook and looking at Annika's name. "And we'll let you know what we find." She put an X though Simio's name on the suspect list.

Blake nodded and hurried ahead to the gorilla cage. When the Aldens got there,

Mr. Newton was already explaining about the mama gorilla, an ape named Harriet. "Gorillas usually only have one baby," Mr. Newton said. He pointed at a leafy nest in the center of the cage. "But sometimes, they can have twins." Up popped two little gorilla heads. "We named the babies Mojo and Jojo."

"Twins!" Griffin and Matthew did a happy dance.

"Just like us," Matthew said.

"Only furrier!" Griffin replied.

"They are so cute!" Annika tossed back her short brown hair before she snapped a picture of the twin gorillas.

"Annika, are you sure you don't have two cameras?" Benny asked her.

"Oh, come on," Annika said, turning to face him. "Is Blake still trying to convince you I stole his?" She waved her camera near Benny's face. "This is my camera! *My* camera!"

"Okay, Annika," Henry said. "Since Blake's is still missing, we needed to check with you."

"Please tell Blake to stop accusing me of taking his," Annika said much more softly. Then she walked away.

"Well, this is a first," Jessie said as she slowly put her notebook in her back pocket.

"A first what?" Benny asked.

"The first time we have crossed off all our suspects and run out of clues before we solved a mystery," Jessie said.

"We can still solve it," Henry told her.

"How?" Violet asked. "Tonight is the pizza party. The zoo tour is almost over!"

"I honestly don't know what we will do," Henry said. "But we can't give up yet."

CHAPTER 8

Pizza Party

By the start of the pizza party, the Aldens hadn't solved the mystery. Blake's camera was still missing.

Jessie opened the door to the Greenfield Zoo Education Center's red barn. The place was decorated with balloons and streamers.

"I smell pepperoni," Benny said. "And veggie pizza. And . . ." He sniffed the air. ". . . a couple of plain cheese pies, too." Benny rubbed his belly and smiled.

"You have an amazing nose," Violet said,

pointing to a table along a side wall. On top of it were the three types of pizzas Benny's nose had predicted.

"Pizza makes every party perfect," Benny told Jessie.

"The only thing that would have made this party better," Henry said, "is if we'd solved the mystery of Blake's missing camera."

Jessie agreed. "I'm disappointed, too. I went over the suspect list a thousand times. I just can't figure it out."

Violet shrugged. "I hope Blake's not too sad at how things turned out. There's still a possibility that one of his other pictures will win."

"Well, I hope one of our pictures wins," Benny said. He grabbed Henry's arm. "Come on, Henry. The pizza's getting cold, and everyone's waiting for me to take the first slice, just like Mr. Newton promised."

The Aldens went to the pizza table and everyone grabbed a few slices, following Benny. Then they sat in the circle of folding chairs.

Matthew and Griffin came to sit beside them. They were dressed in twin zoo shirts with monkeys on them.

"It's a picture of Simio," Matthew told Benny.

"It does kind of look like him," Benny said, leaning in to study the shirt.

"We wanted to always remember that funny monkey," Griffin said.

Sophie joined the circle. She had her blond hair pulled back in a ponytail.

Sophie was wearing her swim charm bracelet. When Mr. Newton showed up, he was wearing his tennis shoes.

"We did solve a few mysteries," Benny told Jessie. "We found a bracelet and a missing shoe!"

Jessie smiled. "I guess it wasn't all bad detective work, huh?"

"No," Violet said. "We did pretty well. Two out of three."

Blake was sitting at the opposite side of the circle. "No one will ever know how great my giraffe picture was," Blake said sadly. "It was an artistic masterpiece!"

"Oh, give it up already," Annika told him. "You lost the camera. The contest results have been decided. Stop complaining."

"I wouldn't complain if you hadn't taken it," Blake said, standing up and waving his pizza crust at her.

"They're fighting again," Violet said to Henry. "Can you get them to stop?"

"I think once Mr. Newton announces the winner, it'll be over," Henry said. "There won't be anything more to argue about."

All the remaining children took seats in the circle. Annika came to sit by the Aldens, as far away from Blake as she could.

"I got all of your photos developed after the tour ended," Mr. Newton said. "The zoologist judges looked at all the pictures. It was hard to decide because there were so many good ones." He took out a zoo pass and held it up. "There is only one grand prize, but today we'll also award second and third place winners."

Mr. Newton asked the kids to make drum roll sounds by patting their hands against their thighs.

"Third place, for his picture of Simio, is . . . Griffin!" Mr. Newton told Griffin to come to the front of the room.

"Thank you," Griffin said, taking a bow. "Third place is good for me!" Mr. Newton gave Griffin a coupon for a free ice cream at the snack bar.

"Oooh," Benny said. "That's a yummy prize!"

"You have to share the cone with me," Matthew told his brother. "It was my camera."

"I do not have to share," Griffin said. "I was the one who took the picture."

"They're as bad as Blake and Annika," Henry whispered to Jessie.

"They are worse," Jessie whispered back. "I bet they fight all day!"

Mr. Newton went on with the presentation. "In second place," he said, "with a shot of her brother and a butterfly on his head is . . . Violet Alden!"

"How'd you know I took the picture?" Violet asked Mr. Newton with a huge smile. "I was sharing the camera with Henry, Jessie, and Benny all day."

Mr. Newton showed her the winning shot. The butterfly was on Benny's head, and Henry and Jessie were in the background of the photo.

"You were the only one not in the picture," Mr. Newton said. "It wasn't too hard to figure out."

"Oh," Violet said with a smile. "Good detective work, Mr. Newton."

"Thanks." Mr. Newton gave Violet a coupon for a supersize popcorn bucket.

"Yippee!" Benny cheered. He held out his hand to take the ticket from Violet.

"No way," she said. "I'm keeping it in my purse. I know you," she winked. "You'll eat the whole thing by yourself."

Benny laughed, rubbing his hands together. "You read my mind," he said.

Mr. Newton brought out an easel that was covered with a sheet. "Here's the grand prize winning photo," he said. "I had a big poster of it made. Are you ready to see?"

The children all got up from their chairs and gathered around.

"And in first place, winning a year pass to the zoo, is . . ." Mr. Newton whipped off the sheet.

Beneath it stood a picture of a baby giraffe,

wobbly on its legs, standing next to its mother.

"Annika Gentry!"

"Oh my gosh!" Annika jumped up and down. She danced around and cheered.

Mr. Newton handed her the zoo pass and a small blue first-place ribbon. "Congratulations," he said, shaking her hand.

"Thanks so much," Annika told him. Annika went over to Benny. "You were my witness!" she said. "Tell Blake that he has to let me be a photographer for the newspaper."

"You made her a deal," Benny said to Blake.

"Oh, fine," Blake said. "I'm not a sore loser. You can take pictures for the paper."

Annika was so excited, she jumped forward, grabbed Blake, and hugged him.

He quickly stepped backwards out of her arms. "No hugging on the newspaper."

Annika laughed.

"I want to see your picture close-up," Blake said, moving through the crowd. "It's good," he started to give Annika a compliment, but stopped. "Mr. Newton!" he called in a loud voice. "Hold everything! Annika didn't win the contest."

The room went silent.

"I won the contest." He pointed at the photograph. "I took this picture!"

CHAPTER 9

Picture Problem

Henry, Jessie, Benny, and Violet rushed over to where Blake and Annika were standing.

"What do you mean?" Benny asked.

"Her name was on the camera, right?" Violet asked Mr. Newton.

"Yes," he said, confused. "I was very careful not to mix up one student's pictures with the others. I'm certain that this photo came from Annika's camera." He squinted at the picture over his glasses. "How do you know it's yours, Blake?"

Blake said, "I know how I framed the shot. I put the tree in the far left corner and the baby's legs in the right. This is my picture. I am positive."

"I was standing next to you," Annika said. "It might be mine."

"No way," Blake told her. "This is not yours!"

"I—"

But before Annika could defend herself, Henry jumped in with an idea. "Mr. Newton, can we see all the pictures from Annika's camera?"

Mr. Newton went to the back of the room and found the envelope that contained her photos. While he was gone, Annika and Blake stood like statues, silently glaring at each other.

Jessie took out her notebook and pen. She wrote down Annika's name on a clean page and next to that, she wrote down Blake's name. Underneath she wrote: "Winning picture?"

Mr. Newton came back with the photos

from Annika's camera. "I would search the pictures myself. But I don't know what you're looking for," he said.

"I'm not exactly sure yet, either, but I'll know when I see it," Henry replied.

Mr. Newton nodded, then handed the envelope of photos to Henry.

Jessie helped Henry. They organized the pictures on the floor by which animals they'd seen during the spring break program. They grouped together the penguins, the giraffes, the butterflies, and all the other animals into small picture piles.

"There are lots of photos," Benny said once Henry and Jessie stepped back from the pictures. "But only one of a giraffe. That was a really great picture. No wonder it won."

"Huh?" Annika said, scanning the photos. "I took lots of giraffe shots. Where are my other pictures?"

Henry's head popped up. "That's it! Benny, you are a genius!"

"I am?" Benny asked. "Oh, right," he added. "I am."

"What do you mean, Henry?" Jessie asked. "Why is it important that there's just one giraffe photo?"

"Because Blake only took one giraffe picture on his camera," Henry explained.

"That doesn't make sense," Annika pointed at some other pictures. "See how I shot the butterflies from many different angles? And I have all these alligator photos?" She touched the pictures as she remembered taking them. "I like to take multiple shots of each animal to be sure I get a good picture."

"That's right," Henry said." He pointed as he explained. "Look carefully. Penguins and giraffes are here." He poked at two photos. "One picture of each. That's all." He pushed those pictures to the side. "Then we had lunch."

Jessie picked up the story from there. "After lunch we saw butterflies." She pointed to the five beautiful pictures of the butterflies. "Then three pictures of hummingbirds. Four of alligators."

"You two somehow switched cameras at

lunch," Henry said to Annika and Blake. He pointed at the first two photos. "Those are Blake's photos from before lunch. He only took one picture of each animal. Then, Annika took pictures after lunch on the same camera. We can tell because there are multiple photos of the same animal."

"How could we have switched cameras?" Blake asked, looking carefully at each of Annika's after-lunch photos. "I had one camera in my bag and the other camera in my hand the whole time."

"Didn't you put the one in your hand on the table at lunch?" Benny asked.

"Good memory!" Violet congratulated Benny. He beamed a happy smile.

"That's when the switch must have happened," Henry said. "When everyone was picking up their cameras."

Annika wasn't smiling. She took a sad, ragged breath. "It looks like Blake really did win the contest." She handed him the zoo pass and the first-place ribbon. "I'm really sorry about the mix-up," she told Blake.

"It's a good picture and you deserve to win."

"Thanks." Blake took the prizes. He smoothed down his red hair with one hand and then went with Mr. Newton to get his photo taken for the zoo newsletter.

"This means we successfully solved another mystery," Henry said to his siblings.

"Wahoo!" Benny cheered.

Jessie closed her notebook. "We did it."

Violet was very quiet.

"What's wrong Violet?" Benny asked.

"Just thinking." Violet turned to Henry, Jessie, and Benny. "At the beginning of the tour, Blake had two cameras and Annika had one. And we always knew where Blake's second camera was. He was saving it in his over-the-shoulder bag for the second day. Right?"

The other Aldens nodded in agreement.

"Then one of Blake's cameras went missing. So he had only one, and Annika still had one. Right?"

Again, her siblings nodded.

"So one camera is still missing. Annika

accidentally took one of Blake's two cameras.
But where did Annika's original camera go?"

CHAPTER 10

Another Mystery to Solve

"That is a good question," Henry told Violet. He went running over to Mr. Newton. "Hey, Mr. Newton, can we see all the pictures from everyone's cameras?"

"I thought the mystery was solved," Mr. Newton said.

"We need to figure out what happened to Annika's camera," Henry explained.

"Ahh," Mr. Newton said, pushing his glasses up with one finger. "I'll go get them. The party's nearly over, anyway. I was going

103

to give the pictures to the students to take home."

Mr. Newton went to get the photographs. When he came back, all the children gathered around as Mr. Newton passed the photos out to each of them.

"I can't wait to see the shots I took," Griffin told Matthew.

"I took better ones," Matthew said to his brother.

Mr. Newton handed the twins two envelopes filled with the pictures from the cameras they shared. The envelopes were both marked Cho on the outside.

As the twins went through them, Henry stood over their shoulder looking. "That's another great one of Simio," he told Griffin, pointing at the photo of the escaped monkey. Henry watched as the boys flipped through all the other pictures. They were able to easily identify which ones each twin took.

"I think it'll make things easier if we go around the room and look for Annika's pictures," Jessie said to Henry.

"Good idea," Henry said.

"Let's split up," Benny suggested. "I'll go over there." He pointed at Nico, who was standing alone, looking at his pictures and giggling. He'd taken off his baseball cap, and each time he laughed, Nico's shaggy hair bounced up and down.

Jessie and Violet each took opposite corners of the room. Henry noticed that Sophie was packing up her stuff, getting ready to leave. He headed over to quickly look at her photos.

"Can I take a look at your pictures?" Henry asked. When Sophie agreed, he took them out of her envelope and flipped through her pile. "You have a bunch of nice giraffe shots," Henry told Sophie.

"Thanks," she said. She took back the pictures and put them away.

A few minutes later, the Aldens got together.

"Nico took silly shots," Benny told the others. "They are mostly of the kids in the tour group, not of zoo animals. So those couldn't be Annika's."

"I didn't find Annika's pictures, either." Henry said to his brother and sisters. "But I did see a lot of really great giraffe pictures. Everyone took some of the baby giraffe. Sophie showed me hers. She had a few that were taken straight on, from about the same place where Violet and I were standing. The baby was looking right at the lens and—"

"Wait a second!" Violet stopped Henry in the middle of his sentence. "Did you say *Sophie* had good giraffe photos?"

"Yes," Henry said. "Pretty ones." He put his hand over his mouth. "Oh no!"

The Aldens looked around the room for Sophie. She was almost out the door. "Stop! Sophie!" Benny shouted. "We need to see your pictures again."

"You already saw them," Sophie said. "My dad's waiting outside."

Jessie said, "It's important."

Violet and Benny stood in the doorway. Henry held out his hand until Sophie gave in, handing him the photos.

"You have lots of giraffe photos, but you

couldn't have possibly taken them, Sophie," Jessie said.

"You didn't have a camera the first day. That's when we saw their habitat," Violet said.

Benny added, "Plus, you don't even like giraffes. You're scared of them!"

Sophie's face turned red. She opened and closed her mouth a few times to talk, but nothing came out. Finally she said, "Oh! I didn't even realize it! These aren't my pictures. They must be Annika's. Mr. Newton, where are my pictures? I don't have any giraffes on mine."

"Those are yours," Mr. Newton said, looking at the photos and the name on the envelope.

"Nope," Sophie said, shaking her head. Her ponytail wiggled. "There must have been another mix-up. I don't like giraffes. These can't be mine."

She tried to hand Mr. Newton the stack of photos, but they fell to the floor with a whoosh.

Henry bent to pick them up. "These are yours, Sophie." He held up a picture of a baby chimp. "There's your swimmer charm, dangling in the corner."

Sophie lowered her eyes. She was caught.

"I am so sorry, Annika," Sophie said. "I didn't mean to take your camera. Honestly. I meant to take Blake's."

"What?!" Blake said, hearing his name and rushing over.

"Well," Sophie began. "It wasn't fair that you got two cameras. I didn't want to enter the contest. I just wanted to have photos for memories." She went on, "So after lunch, when you were putting your sack in the cooler, I took one of yours. They were both in your over-the-shoulder bag, and I snuck one out."

"But Annika had already switched cameras accidentally with Blake. That happened before Blake put the one he was using that day into his bag," Jessie finished. "So the camera you stole was actually Annika's, not Blake's."

Sophie looked down at her shoes. "I feel very bad about the whole thing."

"You shouldn't have stolen Blake's camera," Mr. Newton told Sophie. "Even if you thought it was unfair for him to have two, stealing is wrong."

"I know," Sophie said.

Mr. Newton went out to the front of the zoo to find Sophie's father, Mr. Webb, and explain what had happened.

"I suspected you all along, and I was right," Blake said to Annika. "Well, sort of. You *did* take my camera—"

"But it was an accident," Annika reminded him.

"I know," Blake said. "I'm sorry I accused you of stealing my camera. I looked at the pictures you took, and I have to admit, you are a really good photographer. I'm happy you are going to be a photographer for the school newspaper."

"Really?" Annika asked. "You didn't change your mind, even though yours was actually the winning photo?" She seemed doubtful.

"No," Blake told her. "Welcome to the newspaper staff." They shook hands for the second time.

Sophie's dad came into the room with Mr. Newton.

Sophie rushed up to him. "I'm so sorry, Dad. I took a camera that wasn't mine. And I lied to some kids earlier and said I bought my own. Both things were terribly wrong. I—"

"Whoa," Mr. Webb put his arm around Sophie to slow her down. "I want to understand what happened. Why did you take someone's camera?"

"I knew we couldn't afford one. And I wanted photos for my memory album," Sophie explained. A big tear rolled down her cheek. "I'm really sorry," she said again.

Sophie's dad handed her a tissue. He said, "Maybe you could draw some pictures for the memories. You don't need to spend money to make a moment special."

Sophie nodded and sniffled.

"You are going to need to come up with a way to buy a new camera for Blake," her dad said.

Mr. Newton had a suggestion. "When you aren't swimming, you can come here and help at the zoo," he told Sophie. "We can pay you to clean up trash and look for lost items."

Sophie's dad agreed that it was a good idea.

"Okay," Sophie said, with a big sigh. "I promise I'll work hard."

After Sophie left the zoo with her dad, Annika and Blake thanked Jessie, Henry, Benny, and Violet for their help.

"We were glad to help," Henry said. "And we're happy that we were able to solve the mystery."

"That's right!" Violet said. "We were so close to having our first unsolved mystery."

"But, with all the witnessing and rememberer-ing, we did it!" Benny cheered, "The case of Blake's missing camera is now closed."

* * *

When Grandfather Alden picked up Henry, Violet, Jessie, and Benny, they were bursting with excitement.

"We solved the camera mystery at the zoo!" Benny said proudly. He threw his backpack into the trunk of Grandfather's car.

"Congratulations! You always seem to solve the mysteries you encounter," Grandfather said. He closed the trunk of the car and got into the driver's seat.

When everyone was buckled in and ready to go, Grandfather started the engine. He was about to drive away, when suddenly Mr. Newton came running to the car.

"Benny! Benny!" Mr. Newton shouted. "I forgot to give you something."

"We already have our popcorn prize," Violet told Mr. Newton, as she patted her purse.

"And I got to eat the first piece of pizza like you promised," Benny said.

"This is something different." Mr. Newton reached into his pocket. He pulled out an official zoo employee name tag. Engraved into the badge was the name *Benny Alden.* And under that it said, *Assistant Zoologist.* He handed the badge to Benny.

"You were such a good helper," Mr. Newton said. "Now you have an official title."

Benny grinned while Henry pinned the badge on his T-shirt. "Thanks, Mr. Newton!" Benny cheered. "Can I come back to help again on my next school break?"

"Sure," Mr. Newton said, adjusting his glasses on his nose. "I hope you'll come and bring your brother and sisters, too."

As Grandfather drove the Alden children home, Benny looked at his new badge. "This is better than winning a year's zoo pass," he said. "Much better! I'm an assistant zoologist now!"

Henry, Violet, Jessie, and Grandfather all cheered.

Benny smiled the whole the way home.